USBORNE

FIRST THOUSAND WORDS

IN ENGLISH

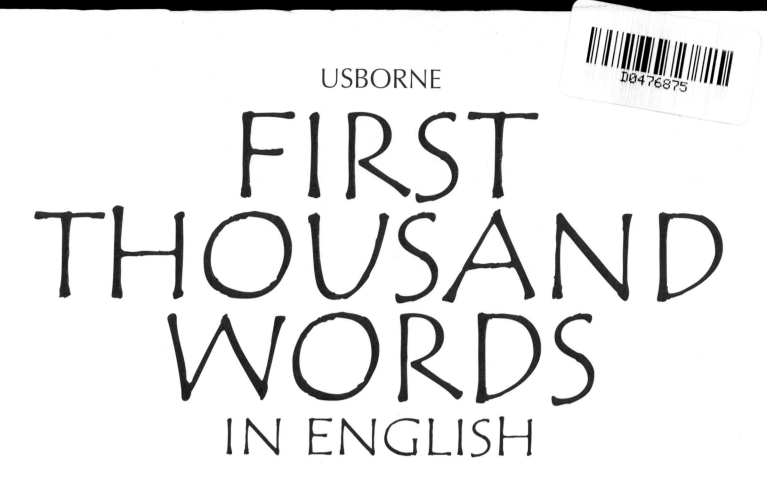

Heather Amery

Illustrated by Stephen Cartwright

Edited by Nicole Irving
and designed by Andy Griffin

On every big picture across two pages,
there is a little yellow duck to look for.
· Can you find it?

About this book

All young children will enjoy this exciting picture word book. Parents and teachers sharing it with them will discover that each page provides lively situations to explore, and to talk and laugh about.

The First Thousand Words is designed to be used at many different levels, so that children of various ages and abilities will find it stimulating and amusing.

At its easiest level, the book can be used as a picture word book for looking and talking. As they grow familiar with favourite pages, children will be able to describe and give names to pictures. Gradually, they can be introduced to the printed words, and, with help and encouragement, they will soon begin matching words with pictures.

Older children can use this book when writing their own stories. It will provide them with ideas, new words and correct spellings.

There is a word list at the back of the book, which brings together all the words in alphabetical order. It can be used to encourage children to look up words and find the right page and picture. This is an important skill, which will prepare children to use simple information books and dictionaries.

Remember, this is a book of a thousand words. It will take time to learn them all!

About this revised edition

This edition brings new life to an enormously popular book. The book has been redesigned to give even clearer pictures and labels, and there are many brand-new illustrations by Stephen Cartwright. The book has also been brought up to date, so that it now includes objects which have made their way into everyday life in recent years.

At home

bath

soap

tap

toilet paper

toothbrush

water

toilet

sponge

washbasin

shower

bed

bathroom

living room

towel

toothpaste

radio

cushion

CD

carpet

sofa

chair

duvet

comb

sheet

rug

wardrobe

pillow

chest of drawers

mirror

brush

lamp

pictures

pegs

telephone

bedroom

hall

radiator

video

newspaper

table

letters

stairs

5

The kitchen

fridge

glasses

clock

stool

teaspoons

switch

washing powder

key

door

vacuum cleaner

saucepans

forks

apron

ironing board

rubbish

sink

kettle

knives

mop

duster

tiles

broom

washing machine

dustpan

drawer

saucers

frying pan

cooker

spoons

plates

iron

tea towel

cups

matches

brush

bowls

cupboard

The garden

wheelbarrow

beehive

snail

bricks

pigeon

spade

ladybird

dustbin

seeds

shed

watering can

worm

flowers

sprinkler

hoe

wasp

bee

trowel

bone

hedge

fork

lawn mower

path

leaves

tree

smoke

caterpillar

rake

bird's nest

sticks

greenhouse

grass

pram

ladder

bonfire

hosepipe

9

The workshop

screws

vice

sandpaper

drill

ladder

saw

sawdust

calendar

tool box

screwdriver

plank

shavings

penknife

10

tacks spider bolts nuts cobweb

barrel

fly

axe

tape measure

hammer

file

paint pot

wood nails workbench jars plane

11

The street

bus

shop

hole

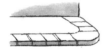
café

ambulance

pavement

aerial

chimney

roof

hotel

man

police car

pipes

drill

school

playground

taxi

crossing

factory

lorry

traffic lights

cinema

van

roller

trailer

house

market

steps

motorcycle

bicycle

fire engine

policeman

car

woman

lamp post

flats

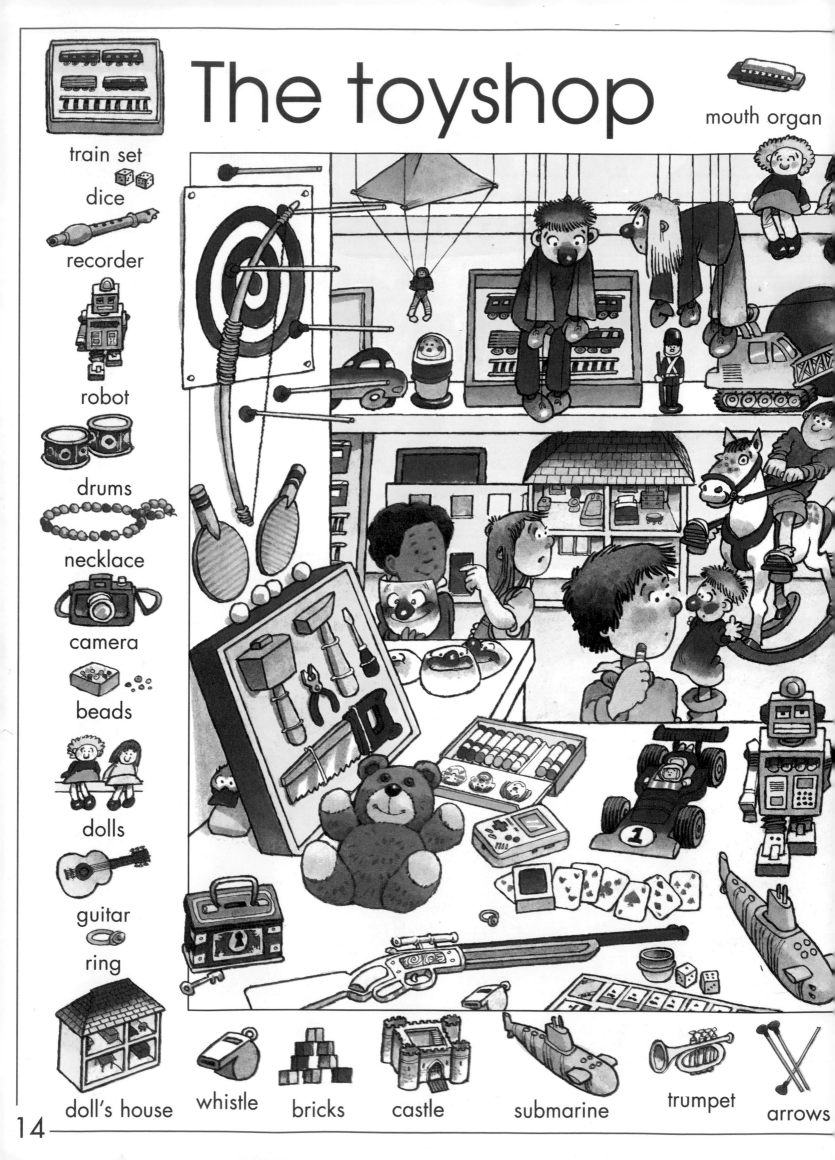

The toyshop

mouth organ

train set

dice

recorder

robot

drums

necklace

camera

beads

dolls

guitar

ring

doll's house

whistle

bricks

castle

submarine

trumpet

arrows

bow   parachute   boat   face paints   roller   masks

racing car

rocking horse

money box

marbles

puppets

piano

spacemen

crane   clay   gun   soldiers   paints   rocket

The park

swings

sandpit

picnic

kite

ice cream

dog

gate

path

frog

slide

bench

tadpoles

lake

roller blades

bush

16

baby

skateboard

earth

push-chair

seesaw

children

tricycle

birds

railings

ball

yacht

string

puddle

ducklings

skipping rope

flower bed

swans

lead

ducks

trees

17

The zoo

panda

wing

eagle

hippopotamus

bat

gorilla

paws

kangaroo

monkey

tail

wolf

iceberg

penguin

crocodile

bear

feathers

pelican

ostrich

dolphin

giraffe

lion

cubs

horns

deer

camel

seal

polar bear

tortoise

trunk

elephant

rhinoceros

bison

beaver

goat

zebra

snake

shark

whale

tiger

leopard

19

Travel

helicopter

The railway station

The garage

railway track

engine

buffers

carriages

train driver

goods train

platform

ticket inspector

suitcase

ticket machine

signals

backpack

headlights

engine

wheel

battery

20

plane

air hostess

runway

control tower

The airport

air steward

pilot

car wash

boot

petrol

breakdown lorry

car wash

petrol pump

petrol tanker

spanner

tyre

bonnet

oil

21

The country

mountain

windmill

hot-air balloon

butterfly

lizard

stones

fox

stream

signpost

hedgehog

lock

squirrel

forest

badger

river

road

tents

canal

logs

village

moth

bridge

barge

waterfall

owl

tunnel

fox cubs

mole

fisherman

rocks

toad

train

caravan

hill

23

The farm

haystack

sheepdog

ducks

lambs

pond

chicks

loft

pigsty

bull

ducklings

hen house

tractor

cockerel

geese

tanker

barn

mud

cart

farmer

field

hens

calf

fence

saddle

cowshed

cow

plough

orchard

stable

piglets

shepherdess

turkeys

scarecrow

hay

sheep

straw bales

horse

pigs

farmhouse

25

The seaside

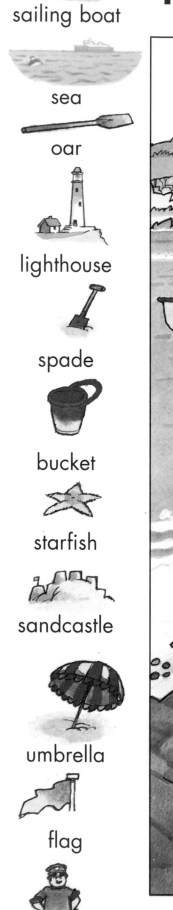

sailing boat

sea

oar

lighthouse

spade

bucket

starfish

sandcastle

umbrella

flag

shell

sailor

crab

seagull

island

motor-boat

water-skier

waves

sunhat

cliff

ship

canoe

rope

pebbles

seaweed

net

paddle

fishing boat

flippers

donkey

fish

swimsuit

oil tanker

beach

rowing boat

deck chair

27

At school

scissors

$$2 + 2 = 4$$
$$3 + 2 = 5$$

sums

rubber

ruler

photographs

felt-tips

drawing pins

paints

boy

pencil

board

desk

books

pen

glue

chalk

drawing

wastepaper bin

teacher

box

map

brush

ceiling

wall

floor

notebook

alphabet

badge

aquarium

paper

blind

easel

door handle

plant

globe

girl

crayons

lamp

abcdefg
hijklmn
opqrstu
vwxyz

The hospital

nurse

cotton wool

medicine

lift

dressing gown

crutches

pills

tray

watch

thermometer

curtain

teddy bear

apple

plaster

bandage

wheelchair

jigsaw

doctor

syringe

The doctor

slippers

computer

sticking plaster

banana

grapes

basket

toys

pear

cards

nappy

walking stick

television   nightdress   pyjamas   orange   tissues   comic   waiting room

The party

presents

balloon

chocolate

sweet

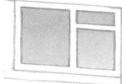

window

fireworks

ribbon

cake   straw   candle   paper chains   toys

clementine

salami

cassette tape

sausage

crisps

fancy dress

cherry

fruit juice

raspberry

strawberry

bulb

sandwich

butter

biscuit

cheese

bread

tablecloth

The shop

grapefruit

carrot

cauliflower

leek

mushroom

cucumber

lemon

celery

apricot

melon

carrier bag

cheese

fruit and vegetables

onion

cabbage

peach

lettuce

peas

tomato

SEGN. 3. VOLTA UK x UK

eggs

plum

flour

scales

jars

meat

pineapple

yoghurt

basket

bottles

handbag

purse

money

tins

potatoes

spinach

beans

checkout

pumpkin

trolley

Food

breakfast

lunch or dinner

boiled egg

toast

jam

coffee

fried egg

cream

milk

cereal

hot chocolate

sugar

honey

salt

pepper

tea

teapot

pancakes

rolls

supper or dinner

ham

soup

omelette

salad

chopsticks

hamburger

chicken

rice

sauce

spaghetti

mashed potatoes

pizza

chips

pudding

Me

head

hair

face

arm

elbow

tummy

toes

foot

leg

knee

eyebrow

eye

nose

cheek

mouth

lips

teeth

tongue

chin

ears

neck

shoulders

chest

back

bottom

hand

thumb

fingers

My clothes

socks

pants

vest

trousers

jeans

T-shirt

skirt

shirt

tie

shorts

tights

dress

jumper

sweatshirt

cardigan

scarf

handkerchief

trainers

shoes

sandals

boots

gloves

belt

buckle

zip

shoelace

buttons

button holes

pockets

coat

jacket

cap

hat

39

People

chef

dancers

actor   actress

singers

astronaut

butcher

policeman

policewoman

carpenter

fireman

artist

judge

mechanics

lorry driver

bus driver

hairdresser

waiter   waitress

postman

dentist

frogman

painter

baker

Families

son
brother

daughter
sister

mother
wife

father
husband

aunt   uncle

cousin

grandfather

grandmother

Doing things

smile

cry

think

listen

laugh

catch

throw

break

paint

write

chop

cut

eat

talk

dig

carry

drink

make

jump

crawl

dance

wash

knit

play

watch

climb

take

skip

fight

sleep

sew

wait

cook

hide

read

buy

push

sing

blow

pull

sweep

pick

fall

walk

run

sit

43

Opposite words

good

bad

far

near

cold

hot

wet

dry

top

bottom

over

under

fat

thin

dirty

clean

small

big

few

many

open

closed

first

last

left

out

in

easy

difficult

empty

full

soft

hard

front

high

slow

fast

back

low

long

short

dead

alive

dark

light

old

upstairs

right

new

downstairs

45

Days

Monday

Tuesday

Wednesday

Thursday

Friday

Saturday

Sunday

calendar

morning

sun

evening

night

space

planet

spaceship

moon

star

telescope

Special days

birthday

present

candle

birthday card

birthday cake

holiday

wedding day

bridesmaid

bride   bridegroom

camera

photographer

Christmas day

reindeer

sleigh

Father Christmas

Christmas tree

Weather

umbrella

rain

lightning

fog

sun

clouds

sky

snow

dew

wind

mist

frost

rainbow

Seasons

spring

summer

autumn

winter

Pets

hamster

guinea pig

vet

kennel

puppy

dog

food

budgerigar

parrot

beak

rabbit

canary

cage

cat

basket

mouse

kitten

milk

goldfish

Sport and exercise

basketball

rowing

snowboarding

sailing

windsurfing

racket

tennis

American football

gym

cricket

karate

bat

ball

baseball

fishing rod

fishing

bait

rugby

dance

diving

swimming pool

swimming

race

archery

target

hang-gliding

jogging

helmet

cycling

climbing

judo

horse

pony

locker

football

riding

changing room

badminton

table tennis

ice skates

ice-skating

ski pole

chairlift

ski

skiing

sumo wrestling

Colours

orange

green

black

grey

red

brown

pink

white   blue   purple   yellow

Shapes

rectangle

circle

diamond

cone

star

cube

oval

triangle

square

crescent

Numbers

1	one	
2	two	
3	three	
4	four	
5	five	
6	six	
7	seven	
8	eight	
9	nine	
10	ten	
11	eleven	
12	twelve	
13	thirteen	
14	fourteen	
15	fifteen	
16	sixteen	
17	seventeen	
18	eighteen	
19	nineteen	
20	twenty	

The fairground

roundabout

mat

helter-skelter

big wheel

hoop-la

ghost train

popcorn

big dipper

rifle range

dodgems

candy floss

The circus

trick cyclist

trapeze

tightrope walker

pole

tightrope

rope ladder

safety net

acrobats

rabbit

juggler

hoop

ring master

dog

top hat

band

bareback rider

bow tie

clown

Words in order

This is a list of all the words in the pictures. They are in the same order as the alphabet. After each word is a number. This is a page number. On that page, you will find the word and a picture.

a

acrobats, 55
actor, 40
actress, 40
aerial, 12
air hostess, 21
airport, 21
air steward, 21
alive, 45
alphabet, 29
ambulance, 12
American football, 50
apple, 30
apricot, 34
apron, 6
aquarium, 29
archery, 51
arm, 38
arrows, 14
artist, 40
astronaut, 40
aunt, 41
autumn, 48
axe, 11

b

baby, 17
back (of body), 38
back (not front), 45
backpack, 20
bad, 44
badge, 29
badger, 22
badminton, 51

bait, 50
baker, 41
ball, 17, 50
balloon, 32
banana, 31
band, 55
bandage, 30
bareback rider, 55
barge, 23
barn, 24
barrel, 11
baseball, 50
basket, 31, 35, 49
basketball, 50
bat (animal), 18
bat (for sport), 50
bath, 4
bathroom, 4
battery, 20
beach, 27
beads, 14
beak, 49
beans, 35
bear, 18, 19, 30
beaver, 19
bed, 4
bedroom, 5
bee, 9
beehive, 8
belt, 39
bench, 16
bicycle, 13
big, 44
big dipper, 54
big wheel, 54
birds, 17
bird's nest, 9
birthday, 47
birthday cake, 47
birthday card, 47
biscuit, 33
bison, 19
black, 52
blind (for a window), 29
blow, 43
blue, 52

board, 28
boat, 15, 26, 27
boiled egg, 36
bolts, 11
bone, 9
bonfire, 9
bonnet (of a car), 21
books, 28
boot (of a car), 21
boots, 39
bottles, 35
bottom (of body), 38
bottom (not top), 44
bow, 15
bowls, 7
bow tie, 55
box, 29
boy, 28
bread, 33
break, 42
breakdown lorry, 21
breakfast, 36
bricks, 8, 14
bride, 47
bridegroom, 47
bridesmaid, 47
bridge, 23
broom, 7
brother, 41
brown, 52
brush, 5, 7, 29
bucket, 26
buckle, 39
budgerigar, 49
buffers (train), 20
bulb (light), 33
bull, 24
bus, 12
bus driver, 41
bush, 16
butcher, 40
butter, 33
butterfly, 22
button holes, 39
buttons, 39
buy, 43

m

make, 42
man, 12
many, 44
map, 29
marbles, 15
market, 13
mashed potatoes, 37
masks, 15
mat, 54
matches, 7
me, 38
meat, 35
mechanics, 40
medicine, 30
melon, 34
milk, 36, 49
mirror, 5
mist, 48
mole, 23
Monday, 46
money, 35
money box, 15
monkey, 18
moon, 46
mop, 7
morning, 46
moth, 23
mother, 41
motor-boat, 26
motorcycle, 13
mountain, 22
mouse, 49
mouth, 38
mouth organ, 14
mud, 24
mushroom, 34
my, 39

n

nails, 11
nappy, 31

near, 44
neck, 38
necklace, 14
net, 27
new, 45
newspaper, 5
night, 46
nightdress, 31
nine, 53
nineteen, 53
nose, 38
notebook, 29
numbers, 53
nurse, 30
nuts, 11

o

oar, 26
oil, 21
oil tanker, 27
old, 45
omelette, 37
one, 53
onion, 34
open, 44
opposite words, 44
orange (colour), 52
orange (fruit), 31
orchard, 25
ostrich, 18
out, 45
oval, 52
over, 44
owl, 23

p

paddle, 27
paint, 42
painter, 41
paint pot, 11
paints, 15, 28
pancakes, 36
panda, 18

pants, 39
paper, 29
paper chains, 32
parachute, 15
park, 16
parrot, 49
party, 32
path, 9, 16
pavement, 12
paws, 18
peach, 34
pear, 31
peas, 34
pebbles, 27
pegs (for clothes), 5
pelican, 18
pen, 28
pencil, 28
penguin, 18
penknife, 10
people, 40
pepper, 36
petrol, 21
petrol pump, 21
petrol tanker, 21
pets, 49
photographer, 47
photographs, 28
piano, 15
pick, 43
picnic, 16
pictures, 5
pigeon, 8
piglets, 25
pigs, 25
pigsty, 24
pillow, 5
pills, 30
pilot, 21
pineapple, 35
pink, 52
pipes, 12
pizza, 37
plane, 11, 21
planet, 46
plank, 10

This revised edition first published in 1995 by
Usborne Publishing Ltd, Usborne House, 83-85
Saffron Hill, London EC1N 8RT.
Based on a previous title first published in 1979.
Copyright © 2002, 1995, 1979 Usborne Publishing Ltd.

Printed in Italy.